OUT OF NOWHERE

ANNIE JOHNSON

MILTON & HUGO L.L.C.
4407 Park Ave., Suite 5
Union City, NJ 07087, USA

Website: *www. miltonandhugo.com*
Hotline: *1- 888-778-0033*
Email: *info@miltonandhugo.com*

Ordering Information:
Quantity sales. Special discounts are granted to corporations, associations, and other organizations. For more information on these discounts, please reach out to the publisher using the contact information provided above.

Library of Congress Control Number:		2025902164
ISBN-13:	979-8-89285-271-5	[Paperback Edition]
	979-8-89285-270-8	[Digital Edition]

Rev. date: 01/14/2025

DEDICATION

I would like to take the time out to thank myself and spirit for giving me nudges to push through and complete this project. This project was in the making for so long, but life happens, and we have to improvise. From one procrastinator to another if I can do it, you can as well. When it comes to your fulfillment and you making your dreams come true the only one that can see you through that is you. So I am so very proud of myself, and I am going to thank myself and celebrate myself every time. If you're not doing that for yourself, it's time to start. Big or small you stepped outside your comfort zone and got the job you wanted completed and done. I love you self, and we did it, girl. Now keep going.

Oh my god, my alarm didn't go off, shit. It's my first day of work. This can't be happening. My transport is already damn near 30mins-1hour away. Okay, stay calm, Audrey. Don't panic, just call in to see if you will still have the job after you tell him you're going to be late.

"Hello, Mr. Anderson, this is Audrey Daniels. I will be running late. My train is having problems right now. Will it be okay if I am running behind a little? Oh great, thank you so much. See you then."

Great, he said he will see me when I make it.

—⧖—

This is the story of Audrey Daniels and the life she thought was so bright.

I had to be at work at 8:00 a.m. It is now 11:00 a.m. I am so going to get fired on my first day, I know it.

Mr. Anderson looks like a coffee junky.

Mr. Anderson says, "Hello, everyone, I am here to tell you what being a part of AT&T team looks like. So you won't be in a cubical answering phones or anything like that, people. This is a hands-on working job. On your application, you said that you love working with people, so in this job, you can show that."

What the fuck is this? One of them door-to-door fucking jobs, isn't it? Say it isn't so. Please not another one.

Mr. Anderson continues, "So you will be in the field every day, going from door to door, to sign these lovely people in the Chicagoland up for the new AT&T Uverse services if they have it in their areas."

That's why he didn't give a fuck if I was late or not. I knew it was too good to be true.

Mr. Anderson says, "Okay, let me introduce everyone from our team before we do the work introduction."

Oh my god, who is this? He is six feet four light skinned, with a tattoo on his neck with a business suit on. He is making me so hot and bothered. He looks so serious and confident. Look at his lips, like a passion for erotic fruitfulness. Oh my god, his skin is so flawless, the way his arms are crossed, and he bit his lip. Oh lord, my panties are getting wet. Audrey, focus.

Mr. Anderson says, "Ms. Daniels, you're next. Can you stand up and introduce yourself to everyone, please."

Audrey introduces herself. "Yes, hello, everyone. My name is Audrey Daniels, and I am looking forward to becoming part of the team."

Mr. Anderson says, "Ms. Daniels, tell us a little bit about yourself."

"All right. I am a fresh college graduate from Chicago State University with my associates in business. And I am new to the work field. No children, just me." *That was so embarrassing. I hate public speaking.*

Mr. Anderson continues, "You will be paired up into teams, and someone will take you out to show you the ropes. So I ask, who is ready to go out and get their first sale? Who is trying to go out and make $400 on sales today? I'm telling you it is possible. Okay, our groups are Darrelle and Audrey, Malcolm and Jasmine, Nettie and Jeremiah, Jessica and Mark."

So now everyone is downstairs picking their areas they are going to patrol, and Mr. Anderson put me with Mr. Right.

Darrelle Jones is so fine. Oh my god, I had to learn how to control my thoughts.

He walks up to me and says, "Audrey, right?"

"Yes, and what's your name again?"

"Darrelle."

"Well, nice to meet you, Darrelle."

We smile.

And he says, "We're going to partner up with Jessica and Mark. Is that okay with you?"

"Well, you'll know if it works or not," I say.

He looks at me and says, "You're feisty, huh?"

I say, "Why do you say that?"

He says, "I can tell. So I see you went to Chicago State. Are you from around there?"

"No, I'm from the low end."

"Well, I am too. I've never seen you before."

"I'm not for everybody to see."

"See, that's what I'm talking about. There you go, being feisty again."

"I'm not trying to be, just stating facts."

"No need to be aggressive with me, sweetheart, with yo thick ass."

I look like I didn't like it, but I love it. I wasn't always the smallest girl around. I have always been plus size but with the right type of curves and hips and a nice stomach, and my face was everything with no makeup. I love me. And I see he is feeling me too.

We got to our first door, and the customer is very rude. Of course, this is Chicago, known for assholes.

So I proceed with a smile and say, "Hello, my name is Audrey, and I am here to offer you a deal on the new AT&T Uverse services in your area today. If you don't mind, can I have a moment of your time to sit down and discuss this with you."

The customer says, "No, you cannot, and don't come and knock on my door tomorrow."

I am so embarrassed and just want to quit right there, but I stuck with the job a few days longer than intended.

—◊—

It is now day 4, and Darrelle and I talk every day, getting to know each other. I find out he is my twin brother and sister's cousin on their father's side, so I go home to talk to their dad about it, and he tells me, "Oh yeah, you be careful and let me know if you need me."

I say, "What do you mean about that?"

And he says, "He can be a pain. Just remember what I said."

I say, "Okay, I will."

I can't get him out my head, and he is such a perfect gentlemen.

My phone text goes off, and it's him saying hi and asking if he can take me to dinner and a movie.

I answer, "Yes, when and where? And I will meet you there."

He says, "No need, I will pick you up. Friday night around seven. Is that good for you?"

And I say, "Yes."

—⚏—

He pulls up in front of my house, and my stepdad tells him to come in. He takes him in the room, and I hear him say, "If you hurt her, I will kill you."

I don't pay any mind because that's what a man says if he feels like you're the father or if they consider you their family, right?

So we go out to his black Range Rover, and he opens the door for me to get in.

I tell him, "Please don't think that because your taking me out that you gon' get some ass."

He says, "That's nice to hear. I don't want a hoe, I want a lady."

And I say, "Okay, just informing."

We go to the AMC downtown to see *Fast Five*. I am really interested in the movie, which I later saw was so good.

He brings the popcorn and drinks.

I tell him, "I am going to go to the restroom. I will be right back."

In the restroom, I'm checking to see how I look. I put some more lip gloss on, and as I am heading out, this girl and her friend are walking in.

The girl says, "I just saw my ex. I hope he didn't see me."

The other girl says, "Who?"

"Darrelle. I'm glad I left his ass."

I smile and say, "Excuse me."

I am back in my seat, so I tell him, "You're bumping into exes here. I hope you don't bring every girl here."

He says, "Naw, none of my exes are here."

So I think, *Maybe she meant someone else.*

We're watching the movie, and he puts his arms around me, and I lay on his chest. I feel so comfortable and safe. I remind myself to take things slow.

After the movie, we go to the Grand Lux restaurant, which is expensive.

I ask him, "I know you don't make money to spend at that job for somewhere like this."

He says, "No, I do construction on the side with my uncle. He owns his own construction company."

I tell him, "Because I don't date drug dealers."

He says, "I know, you look like you don't, and that is why I gotta have you."

I tell him, "If you can stick around long enough, we will see."

—∞—

I quit the AT&T job, of course. He is helping provide for everything for me. I still live at home with my mother, and I don't plan on leaving anytime soon. He is everything. He is kind, nice, polite, and respectful. He pays for everything and is even making the payments for my student loans while I am looking for other work. He tells me I don't have to ever work if I am going to be his woman. I have met all of his friends. I don't want to meet his family because I know my stepfather's family and feel they are all just messy, so I am not interested.

—∞—

So we're six months in now, so I decide tonight is the night. So with the money he had given me to go shopping, I buy some lingerie and book a room at the Hyatt on Wacker Drive.

I call and say, "I have plans tonight for us, so make sure you come and get me around 8:00 p.m."

He says, "Make it seven thirty, baby."

—∞—

So he pulls up and sees me in my little red dress, and I mean, it was little and in some heels I could barely walk in. He greets me with a handful of my ass and a kiss like he knows I am on the menu for tonight. He looks so good and dresses even better. His scent drives me crazy, and his touch makes me insane. I feel like I want this moment to last forever. So I had my bestie, Erica, set up candles and rose petals everywhere. I text her to let her know when to be out.

So as we're getting in the car I tell him to let me drive tonight and he has to be blindfolded on the way there. He agrees. We laugh and talk the whole way there, and I take the blindfold off as I pull up to the valet.

He is like, "Baby, why are we at the Hyatt?"

And I'm like, "I want tonight to be special."

He says, "Seriously?"

And I'm like, "Yes, of course."

He says, "Why didn't you let me plan this for you?"

I tell him, "You already do so much. Let me do something, and besides you paid for it, let me try to bring you some joy with surprises this time."

We are on the elevator, and he grabs me and says, "I never had anyone make me feel the way you do. One day you're going to be my wife." Then he gives me the best sloppiest kiss I ever had, and I'm turned on, loving every minute of this.

In the elevator, my dress is almost up, and we are in tuned emotionally, spiritually, and physically in that moment. We hear it's our floor, and we hurry to race off the elevator.

I tell him to close his eyes now that we are in front of the door. I open it and let him look. Erica did so well. She had everything in a perfect setting. We take our shoes off at the door to walk across red and white rose petals, and they are all on the bed, and a dinner for two is placed on the table, with candles and strawberries with champagne.

He is so stunned by what I have done that it turned him definitely on. I tell him that I really care about him and I want him to know that and feel it. He says that he really cares about me too. He lays me on the bed, taking off my thong with his teeth. He kisses my foot up my leg into my thigh and around my pussy and then he licks me so soft and gentle. My soft and sexy moans turn him on even more, and he turns me over and kisses my ass. He grabs it and kisses and licks. That is a surprise for me, but it feels amazing. So now he turns me back over and kisses my stomach and kisses my neck. I am like, *Thank god, he didn't kiss me in my mouth.* And he is sucking on my nipples. I am on fire and so ready for any and everything at this point. I have reached the highest of my sex drive as I have never done before.

He looks at me and says, "I love you," as he inserts his big dick in my pearl-rosy pussy.

I am surprised by how big he is, and I kiss him and say, "I love you too," not knowing that trouble will follow after the magical three words.

At that moment and time in my life, that is the best sex I ever had. I came ten times in one hour. I am in heaven on earth. No complaints or energy from me. I go to sleep right after.

—m—

He wakes me up about four hours later and asks me to shower with him. He has the shower running and some old-school Luther Vandross song "Always and Forever" on. I take a sip of water before proceeding with him to the shower. He kisses my shoulder and takes the soul from my body and helps me to step into the shower. He gets the sponge and squeezes water onto my chest as he sucks on my nipples. I decide to return the pleasurable favor, and I kiss his chest, going down, inserting his nut sack into my mouth and going up, sucking his dick, deep throating until he comes with the water running over my head. I messed my silk press up.

He gets out, and I shower before returning to bed.

He says, "Come to the table, my love. You have to eat."

I pout and say, "Really? Do I have to? I'm tired."

He says, "Yes, I have to make sure you're satisfied all around. No excuses. You're mine now."

So we sit with the candles still burning, talking and enjoying our steak and potatoes.

He says, "I have a surprise for you later today."

I say, "Really, no, bay, you already do too much, really."

He say, "Okay, I can promise that just for today I won't buy any gifts, but I do still have a surprise for you."

I giggle and say, "Okay."

He looks at me and says, "You're so beautiful. How did I get so lucky?"

I say, "I don't know, it must have been according to universal plans for our paths to connect."

He takes the whipped cream and pours it into my mouth and kisses me from my lips to my hips, and I tell him to just go deep.

Three hours later, we are like in a coma, sleeping.

—⁂—

His phone rings.

I tell him, "Bay, get up and get that."

He doesn't budge.

I wake him more persistently, and he wakes up and answers the phone.

We then took a shower, got dressed, and headed out for the day.

He tells the receptionist at the lobby, "We won't be staying for the extra day that was booked."

I ask him, "Why?"

He says, "Because I have a surprise. This time it's my turn."

I smile and say, "Okay."

He drops me off at my mom's house and tells me he will be back at 4:00 p.m., so I should be ready.

I come in and see my mom in the kitchen cooking.

She says, "Girl, I didn't see you come in last night. Does that mean you finally gave him some."

I say, "Mom, too much information dang nasty."

She says, "I hope you know what you are doing with that one. I see the expensive things he buys, and he takes you out every night. Is he a drug dealer?"

I tell her, "No, he does construction with his uncle, and he has another commission-paying job."

She says, "Okay, that's what they tell you in the beginning, girl. In your room there is a big box on your bed that was dropped off for you yesterday after you left. It was hand delivered because don't no delivery man runs that late."

I say, "Okay, Mom. Thanks."

She is always so negative when it comes to who I date. She doesn't think no one is good enough for her girls. There are five of us, and I am the baby girl. They all get on my nerves. My oldest sister is Keisha. She's married with four kids. I think it's too many for me to count, but she and her husband are very happy, and I love that. The second sister is messy Diana in the dictionary after Messy is Diana Daniels. She is always in someone's business. She is single and always ready to mingle and not for free with two kids, and my momma still doesn't know that her daughter is a hoe. The third sister is Steph, short for Stephanie. She's the kind one out of all of us. Sometimes she's too kind. I'm trying to fix that in her. She's married with a nothing-ass husband and one baby girl. I love her so much. The fourth sister is Kiara. After fighting in the dictionary is Kiara Daniels. We always in fights because of her. She's a stripper, and she doesn't care. My mother hates what she does. She tries to tell my mom she is in school working on her masters in business, but she is stripping to take care of the cost for school. She doesn't have any kids. And then there's me, Audrey Daniels, the baby girl just graduated from college and no kids.

I guess you can say I'm cold. I have zero tolerance for the bullshit, and I'm a bit emotionless, and that's why it is a surprise when I told him that I love him back. See, in my past relationships, that doesn't happen. When a guy I'm dating gets to the I love you part, it usually ends up with me breaking up with them, and then I'm the heartless bitch of America. So Darrelle is my first love, I guess you can say. And he doesn't even know it.

So I look at my bed, and there's this big white box with purple ribbon on it. See, purple is my favorite color, and Darrelle knows that. Every gift he has ever given me comes with purple ribbon. I pulled the ribbon to open the box, and I see it is a very beautiful nice, flowy but sexy fitted black dress with some silver-red bottoms. This is by far was the most expensive present he has ever given me. I think my plans for last night upped the ante.

There's a note that says, "I have a surprise for you, and you will wear me."

I call him to say thank you and tell him, "I thought I said no gifts."

He says, "That was before I promised." Then he tells me to just make sure I am wearing it before he comes to pick me up.

I definitely need my hair done, so I go to my beautician, Michelle. She is the gossip queen.

I ask her, "Please squeeze me in as I have a hot date in an hour."

She says, "With Darrelle?"

I tell her, "Yes."

She says, "He already booked me for you. And after, you go next door for a polish change. He already called and paid for everything. Girl, he is a keeper."

I tell her, "Girl, I know."

—⟨⟨⟩⟨—

So about an hour and a half or two later, he calls to see if I was still at the shop. I tell him yes. He says he is on his way to come and pick me up. My friend is just wrapping up with my lashes.

So I hurry to change in the salon's bathroom before he comes.

All the heads in the shop turn as he walks in to escort me, and I tell Michelle, "Bye."

She says, "I will call you later, Audrey," with a frown on her face.

He opens my door, and I get in the car excited.

"Babe, where you are taking me."

He says, "It's a surprise, remember? Don't ruin it."

I say, "Okay."

He takes us to country club hills. We pull up in the driveway, and I say, "Whose house is this?"

He says, "Baby, there is something that I have to tell you."

I say, "Okay," with a pause of concern.

He says, "We're in the next phase of our relationship, and I feel that you're going to be it for me. I have never done this before, but this is my mother's house, and my family is having a fundraiser tonight. I brought you to the house to meet them before we head to the hall for the fundraiser."

Oh my god, I don't like meeting families. It's just too much pressure, and this time I really care, so I don't want to make a bad impression on his family. My knees instantly get weak, and my mouth becomes dry.

I say, "Okay, honey. I hope I don't screw this up."

He says, "As lovely as you are, you can't, and even if you do, I have already picked you."

I kiss him and take a deep breath, and we go in.

—⁂—

His mother is Black. She looks like she hasn't aged at all. His stepfather is White and nice. But his mother turns her nose up at me. He has two sisters, Jane and Gabriella, and a brother named Ar'mon, who almost looked as good as he did. I shake everyone's hand, introducing myself as Audrey.

"I'm his friend," I say. I feel we are too grown to say "boyfriend and girlfriend" at age twenty-two and twenty-five.

So his mother asks, "What do you plan to do with your life?"

She is straight to the fucking point. I am highly irritated by her, but I can't blame her. It looks like they are wealthy, and she wants to make sure I am not using him.

So I tell her, "I am a recent graduate, and I am looking for work, but I do want to open my own business one day, a shelter to help the homeless and a massive bed and breakfast, but I don't want it to be a hotel so that I could build myself a house from the ground up. But right now I'm still home with my parents."

She turns her nose up, saying, "Get your own place, honey. You mean to tell me you're still at home with your parents, assuming they're in one household."

I look at Darrelle to show him how uncomfortable I have become and want his help getting out of this situation.

So he says, "Mom, don't you think you're being too personal?"

Her husband intervenes and asks her to help him in the kitchen.

I tell Darrelle, "Are you sure we have to go to the fundraiser tonight?"

He states that it is very important to his family and now that I am being considered to become a part of it, I need to be onboard with these events. He pleads, "Please, honey."

I say, "Okay, but only for you."

His sister Jane is messy like my sister Diana, Gariella is sweet, and Ar'mon is flirtatious.

Jane proceeds to say, "So you know what he really does, right?"

I tell her, "Yes, he works for his uncle doing construction and he's a sales rep for AT&T."

She chuckles and says, "Honey, he doesn't like you that much. He didn't even tell you what he does. He owns those companies."

I go back in to speak to him, to see what it is that she's talking about, but we are about to head up the street to the fundraiser for the event. So I am furious but decide this isn't the time or place. I don't want to ruin what is important to his family, even though I don't really like them so far.

We all pull up to the valet.

He asks, "What is wrong?"

I am quiet on the way over. I just tell him, "My stomach feels unsettling."

—m—

Up ahead is the red carpet. It is a breast cancer awareness fundraiser, which made me feel a bit better, being there for a great cause. I walk into a place that I have only seen in movies, and it doesn't look big on the outside. It is very private and secluded.

As we walk in, I see a lot of recognizable faces but not have seen in person. I turn to see Trey Songz, Adele, Beyonce, Jay-Z, Oprah, and many more A-listers. That explains the expensive outfit and shoes. And everyone knows him and his family. I see why his mom was grilling me now. Shit, if I get to be around them occasionally, I would grill me too. And everyone mingled with us because of Rell. That is how they addressed him.

Oprah walks over and proceeds to shake my hand. She says, "Rell, who is this beautiful young lady?"

My mouth suddenly gets dry as I am shocked and at lost for words as Oprah Winfrey just said that I am beautiful and that she is interested in getting to know me.

I respond, "Hello, thank you so much. It is a pleasure to meet you. I am Audrey Daniels."

She states, "The pleasure is all mine." Then she tells Darrelle, "You know with a women this naturally beautiful with no makeup puts ever woman tonight with a face to shame and a beautiful personality to match. Rell, don't leave her on the market too long. You both enjoy your evening. Hope to see you soon as Mrs. Jones instead of Ms. Daniels."

I smile and say to Darrelle, "She is great. How do you know all these people? Why didn't you tell me they would be here?"

"It was a surprise. I knew that you would love it."

"Okay, so tell me about this event. How did it all come about? Who thought of it?"

So he says that he started it because their aunt Lucy died of breast cancer. She was his mom's best friend, and she was a bit depressed after she died, so he founded the Lucy Foundation and asked some people he knew to come together to think about how many lives are lost to breast cancer yearly and they all will make donations for programs to help find cures.

So completely amazed, I passionately kiss him. We proceed to our table with a plate of nicely decorated expensive chicken with artichoke gravy with a fancy pasta and with a $3,000 bottle of champagne.

I put on all the elegance I had that night. It is a nice event. There was entertainment and informative information about cancer and slide shows of the celebrities volunteering and making donations that they never show on TV.

So a month ago, he promised to take me out, but he canceled because of a prior engagement that he had made and that I made him forget, he said.

"Now you will see what I was doing last month."

He pops up on this screen with this beautiful baby girl and her parents. He was playing games with her, and he donated $50,000 to the family. I am in awe. I look at him and smile and tell him that was beautiful, giving him a face full of kisses that touches me and makes me emotional.

—⁂—

Now it's the end of the night, and we're saying our goodbyes. He opens my door, and we're in the car, and he says, "I have one more surprise."

All these months we have been everywhere, but I have never once been to his home. I am not even thinking about the surprise as I have so many questions going on in my head, like his sister was right. How did he donate $50,000? How does he know these celebrities? Is he a millionaire? I asked spirit how in the hell did I get this lucky and why didn't anyone that knew tell me?

He looks over and stares while driving. He says, "Honey, don't fall asleep, we will be there soon, okay?"

I sigh and say, "Okay."

It is like fifteen minutes later, and we enter a gate, but now he is driving for five more minutes, and you can't see anything but trees and grass, nice grass. Now we are reaching the end of the road to pull up in front of this massive deserted mansion.

He says, "Welcome to my home."

It is beautiful. It is the type of house that doesn't even exist, like they would have to do the green screen for it in the movies. I am stunned by how beautiful it is. I couldn't believe it. After I thought I knew someone and we are becoming closer, to find out that I don't know him at all. But in the moment of so many emotions, the presentation doesn't appeal to me in that moment like it should have because I am in the dark on who he really is.

I am pissed, and he sees it. He opens my door, to only see the disappointment on my face.

He says, "Honey, what's wrong? What did I do?"

I cry. I don't really know why I did, but I did. And I say, "You lied to me. Why? Who are you? Did you think you can bring me up here, and I would just be so fascinated by your house that I wouldn't ask questions that really matters. How were you able to donate $50,000 to that family? How are you able to afford this house? So you work as a sales rep and a construction worker and can afford all of this. I'm not buying it, so please don't lie to me anymore. I was honest with you. I let you in. You were the only person who ever got to see the real me, and now to find out that I don't even know who you are at all."

"Baby, please just let me explain. Okay, it was like you were the only person on the planet who didn't know who me and my family were. We try to keep who we are anonymous, but that doesn't always happen. My name is Darrelle Jones. I didn't lie to you about that. My father was an architect, and he owned his own architectural firm. He died and left everything to me, his firstborn son. He left a note to me telling me to expand and explore and to make my family rich and to forever take care of them because my mother would drive the business into the ground and my siblings weren't mature or old enough at the time. But I couldn't receive any of the rights to the business without completing my BA at least in entrepreneurship so that I will know how to start something from the ground up, so I did, at age twenty-three. At twenty-two, I had ownership over the entire architectural firm, and I started a construction company for my brother and uncle to run. I started a day-care centers with three sites for my sister Gariella to run, and Jane is in charge of six salons all over Chicagoland and is about to open a new one in Englewood. And at AT&T, they gave me the opportunity to partner with them and open a few locations. So, honey, I didn't tell you the truth because I had to see if you were really for me or for my money. And now I see that you're all for me, so how could I not share everything with you? I promise that from here on out, there will be no more holding back or lies. I love you. And for what you did the other day at the hotel, no one has ever tried to show me that they appreciate me. People are usually trying to use me, but I'm too smart for that. Honey, I love you so much, and I am ready to be all in with you. Do you forgive me? Please forgive me."

I wipe my face and looked at him and say, "No more lies," and I kiss him and forgive him. So now I'm like, "Okay, show me your house."

I tell him before we enter the house, "I don't care how rich you are. I'm going to always want to work. Don't try to stop me from doing that. I will not get caught up in your world where I will lose myself. I'm not that girl. Are you willing to accept that from me right before we enter this door?"

He says, "Hell, yeah. Get over here."

We kiss.

As we enter, there is a double staircase with this beautiful fountain in the center. I have never seen anything like it. As we walk up the stairs to the master suite, I am nervous to have found out everything that I did, and I am about to have sex in a mansion. It doesn't get more nerve-racking than that.

As we walk in the bedroom, my mouth drops. It is so beautiful. There are big beautiful windows, no curtains. The color scheme is gold, black, and white. There is a hot tub a ways from the bed in which purple rose petals are everywhere, in the hot tub, on the bed, there are candles everywhere. It is beautiful. I cry. I realize that I have been a crybaby that whole night. I haven't cried that much in a long time. I just am not an emotional person, but with him, he brings out all my emotions.

I sit on the couch, and he says, "Honey, are you okay?"

I reply, "No one has ever cared this much for me."

And he says, "And no one has for me like you do."

We kiss, and he's gently takes off my shoes. He turns on Luther, and with my hand into his, he pulls me up to hold me to his chest, and we dance. In that moment, I feel like a princess. and he is my knight and shining armor.

He whispers in my ear, "I'm going to make an honest woman out of you very soon. You just wait for me, please."

In a moment of silence and just embracing each other, we feel like we are on cloud nine. He turns me around to unzip my dress and takes off my undergarments. I repay the favor to undress him.

Oh lord, a man this fine and successful. I can't believe he wants me and that he is mine. Undoing his pants, I start kissing his lower stomach and around his penis. I lick his balls and inserted his penis into my mouth and hummed with the head at the back of my throat. He yelled a bit from a confusing satisfaction of sexual pleasure. I continue to suck back and forth, very slowly for a few minutes, and I kiss the tip. He picks me up off my feet and walks to the hot tub. We get in and make very passionate love in the bedroom that night.

—∿—

His alarm is going off at 6:00 a.m. I am awakened on his chest on the couch. We never made it to the bed. He has to get ready for work.

His maid knocks at the door. "Are you decent, Mr. Jones."

He says, "Give me five minutes, Lesil."

She enters, and he says, "Have Leon cancel all my plans for the day. I will be having quality time with my love today, and do everything for breakfast please."

Wrapped in a satin silk sheet, I go to use the gigantic bathroom, which leads to a patio area. I go out on the patio and just close my eyes and listen to the wind and nature. I let the wind blow through my hair. In that moment, I am the happiest I have ever been in my life. I am in a reality experience of a fairy tale.

Darrelle wonders what is taking Audrey so long, only to find her on the patio with her eyes close, just embracing the surroundings. In his sight is the most beautiful and humble woman he has ever come across in his life. Darrelle can't understand, after all the years and relationships he's ever been in, how come he's just met Audrey now? He wonders why God sent her at this time in his life. Well, he doesn't care anymore. He just wants to appreciate every moment spent together. He slowly walks up to her and wraps his arms around her and embraces the sweet and soft body. Touching her made everything make sense, and his body intensifies with high electric sexual drive.

He whispers in her ear, "Do you understand how beautiful of a person you truly are. You're amazing."

She replies, "Well, thank you, Mr. Jones. You ain't too bad yourself."

And they giggle.

"So what's on the agenda today, honey," Audrey says with a spunk.

Darrelle replies, "I hope, you."

She says, "No, we're not staying in, having sex all day. We need to do something fun and priceless. I have an idea. I know where we're going. It's super casual, and you will feel great after, and then I will need you to try and continue to put this in your schedule as often as you can. I hope you're ready to meet some really amazing people today."

He replies, "So what is that we're doing?"

She answers, "We are helping you to appreciate your accomplishments and this big ole house."

—⚉—

In the car, on the way to wherever she was taking us to, she told Darrelle a story.

"I had a friend in high school, my first best friend, and her name was Amber. She would study with me. We would go out together and have fun like the average teenagers, and we always had sleepovers at my house. I would ask her to check with her parents to make sure it was fine. My mom would always call her mom to make sure it was okay, and I would always pay for everything because I was more of the adventurous one, so it was always me wanting to go, and I was blessed that my parents could provide for me to do those things. So one day I said, 'Amber, can you call your mom and see if we can spend a night at your house tonight because my mom is really getting on my nerves today.' So she replied, 'We can't, but your my best friend, I can't keep lying to you, so we're going to go to my home. I can trust you, can I?' And I said, 'Of course, you're my sister.' We get on the bus and go downtown, and I'm like, 'Dang, we're downtown.' Her parents must have really nice jobs, until I see where we are going, a building that's for homeless people, and she says, 'I just have to ask Ms. Jenkins a questions first.' So I'm like, 'Okay.' She says, 'Ms. Jenkins said it's okay to show you where I sleep, but we have to be quick.' In that moment, my heart dropped. I couldn't believe that all this time she was homeless, my best friend who never seem I never knew. So she told me about how her parents died in a fire when they fought with each other. Her dad took her downstairs to the neighbors out the building and set the building on fire with all the other tenants in it. So the neighbor kept her, but she was old and died, so that left her a homeless teenager. She didn't want to go into the system, so she went to school, shoplifted, and slept at shelters here and there. Then she found out about the Chicago Coalition, and it became her home. With tears in her eyes, my best friend committed suicide because someone found out about her situation at school, and they bullied her. She never said a word to me about it. When she did it, she left me a note and told me everything that was bothering her. She said that I was the only thing that kept her going. She said I was a good person, and I never judged her and always made her feel welcome and at home."

Darrelle makes Audrey pull over and holds her weeping head and just let her cry.

She says, "No matter how successful I become, I have to stay humble for Amber."

She took them to the Chicago Coalition for the Homeless. It was Amber's home, a complete 360 from what he is expecting from her. She always amazes him and does something unexpected to where he can't keep track.

She says, "Why not spend a day putting our time together to some good use and take a break and get back to the real."

They go to the outreach center where the teenagers talk to some of the kids in the center and hear their stories and see if there is anything they could help them with.

Darrelle thinks it will be great to make a list of things that they needed, whether it be a need or want. Then they go to the nearest Target to pick up the items for a few of the teens.

They have such an amazing time getting to know the kids and hearing their stories.

Darrelle feels there is something more that he can do for the children in this situation.

—⚅—

On our way home, Darrelle brainstorms all his ideas with her, about opening a homeless shelter for teenagers and naming it in honor of her friend Amber.

"And if you want, you can have complete and total control as long as I can be a volunteer."

She looks at Darrelle in silence for about a minute in a half. He doesn't expect that type of reaction until she screams and says, "Yes, oh my gosh, oh my gosh, oh my gosh, are you serious right now?"

She is so ecstatic. She lights up from the idea, and Darrelle is so happy. He tells her that it can take awhile before they find a place, or if they have to build a place, he will have to go over the funding and everything.

"My manager is not going to be happy about this, but it's my money."

Audrey cries and says, "Thank you so much. You don't know how much this means to me."

He replies, "I think I do. Audrey, hear me out. I know we haven't known each other that long, but I feel so drawn to you, and I can't imagine living life without you. *Will you marry me?*"

Her face lights up, and she replies, "Wow, I never thought I would get married—"

"Audrey," Darrelle says, "Audrey—"

"Let me finish, honey. But then I never thought that I would meet someone like you. You help me to be a better me. You make me feel alive, like I am so emotional but in a good way. So, *yes, yes*, I will marry you, because of us being together, we are better.

Darrelle cries tears of joy, kissing Audrey's face all over.

She cries and looks at him and says, "You're first love and only love. Did you really think I was going to say no?" She giggles.

He says, "After you didn't immediately say yes, I thought maybe you were thinking it's too early."

Audrey says, "You can't put a time on true love."

They go home that day and stay in and make fireworks happen for hours.

—·w·—

She wakes up the next morning to him watching her while she is asleep. He kisses her on her forehead and suggests breakfast in bed and that they needed to talk about something from his past.

He says, "Your phone is going off."

She looks at it, and it is Michelle, and she has called four times and left a voice mail. She texted, "Darrelle murdered his ex-girlfriend."

Audrey looks at Darrelle, and she can't believe what she is seeing right now.

He smiles and kisses her on her forehead and asks if she wanted breakfast.

She is terrified and tries to play it cool. She thinks she knows him better than anyone, but he did lie about being rich.

She is scared, so she says, "What we have to talk about, is it bad?"

With a pause, he says, "Nah, not really. It's about a past friendship."

So now Audrey is freaking out, and she's like, *Oh my god, she was right.*

So she starts putting on her clothes and states that she needed to go home right away, that she forgot she had to babysit her niece and if she doesn't hurry, her sister will miss her flight.

Panicky, she says, "Oh my god, honey, I don't know how I forgot to tell you. We need to hurry."

So Darrelle gets up to take her, and she's like, "Honey, you have so much to do. Can you just have your driver take me, and I will call you later, and I will have her for five days. I really don't know how I forgot to mention it to you."

So they do not get to have the talk about his past. She is too afraid for him to tell her and more so afraid of becoming his next victim. So she gets in the car.

And then he calls and says, "Baby, you are acting pretty funny, is everything okay?"

She says, "Yes, I just completely forgot, and that was who was calling me, my sister."

In that moment, he knows she had just lied to him, but he didn't understand why. Because he had looked at her phone and saw it was Michelle, not her sister. He doesn't understand why she would lie about that.

So he says, "Okay, baby, you have a great day. And I will see you later. I love you."

And she pauses with such sadness and replies, "I love you more."

She has so much going on in her head she doesn't know what to think or what to do. She tells the driver to drop her at the salon so that she could hear what Michelle knows about the situation.

Walking in, it is 7:00 a.m. and luckily, Michelle doesn't have any clients yet.

Sad and devastated, she asks Michelle if they can talk in her car to further explain what she said to her.

Michelle hugs her tightly, and they get in the car.

"Michelle, please tell me what you texted me isn't true. I just left his house in a panic. I didn't know what to do. I love him.

Michelle says, "His ex was my husband's baby cousin, and her husband was king drug dealer. They were dating for a few months three years ago, and then she got strung out on drugs, and she was never seen after."

Audrey asks, "So do you all even know if she's dead or not?"

"No, we don't, but how do you explain it. He's rich, and he has the power to make her disappear, and that's who she was with at the time. She's been missing for three years, Audrey."

Audrey gets out of the car unsure of everything that was told to her. She is thinking that he was probably trying to tell me what happened but she didn't let him.

Still unsure of what to do, Audrey goes home and cries and vomits in the garbage can for hours. She finally gets up to a phone call from Darrelle she has ignored. He left a voice mail.

She texts him, saying, "Honey, I just want to spend time with my niece for these five days at home. Is that okay?"

He answers, "Of course, after all we have a lifetime, right?"

She says, "Yes, we do."

He says, "Besides, I can catch up on work and do the introduction for the business proposition that we talked about, Amber."

She says, "Okay, I love you."

He says, "I love you more, my queen."

—⚭—

Three days goes by, and she gets the occasional text from Darrelle, and she responds just enough for him not to worry, but he feels something is off with her.

She hasn't eaten anything and barely bathed.

Her stepfather knocks on her door to see if she wants to talk.

She tells him to come in.

He sits on the end of her bed, and he says, "What's wrong, baby girl? You haven't been yourself lately."

She cries and says, "Why didn't you tell me about the girl that went missing? Is that why you threatened him when he first took me out? How could you know and not tell me, Dad? I love him."

Her stepfather is so sad and feels so sorry for her. He wipes her face and tells her to calm down and he is going to say his peace.

"Baby girl, look at me. Did he tell you what happened?"

She sniffs and says, "No. I think he was about to tell me, but then Michelle texted me, telling me he killed her, so I hurried up and got out of his house."

He says, "Stop listening to that gossiping Michelle from the salon and give him the opportunity to speak his peace.

"But things are not what they seem."

Her stepfather says, "What I said that day on your first date was because, even though you are not technically my daughter and he's family, I had to let him know that he don't get a free pass to hurt my little princess. No matter how old you are, you're still my little girl. I have been with you since you were one years old, and I will continue to be here with your crazy mother. I love you."

Audrey cries in her father's arms.

—⚬—

An hour pass, and she showers and eats dinner with her family. She feels much better, thanks to her stepfather. But she still doesn't know how to go about things with Darrelle.

—◊◊◊—

In the middle of a family movie night, to help cheer her up, there is a knock at the door. Her stepfather calls her name. It is Darrelle with some lilies, her favorite flower, in shining purple paper. Her stepfather called him because he felt that they needed to talk, to get things squared away.

She goes outside to his car, and there is a dead silence for about thirty seconds.

He says, "Honey, I know why you lied to me about babysitting your niece and why you didn't want to be around me. My cousin told me what Michelle told you. I was going to talk to you about it that morning, but you just took off. So now can you please give me the opportunity to tell you what happened?"

She says, "Okay, I'm listening."

Darrelle says, "So three years ago, I went to a bar late after work and met this girl. She was pretty, and she was sloppy drunk, so I was uninterested, but she was very interested. So we sat and talked for a while, and I got tipsy, and so we took a cab to her house, and one thing lead to another. I considered her to be a friend at the time. I wasn't trying to be serious with anyone. I had so much going on trying to learn the business fresh out of college, and we established a friendship, and she will tell you that. She was secretly dating this guy named Eric that worker for her cousin Michelle's husband, and he was a drug dealer. She would always call me right before she passed out from being so high, so I would go over to help her out for a couple days. She said that if her family found out, they would kill him, and I told her that they should but that she was grown and she made the decision to start even though he is in the wrong. This was the first, then it became a tenth in ten months. She became unrecognizable. Her family cut her off. So she asked me the very last time when she was high that if she didn't die in that moment, would I help her to get her life together and could I promised her that no one would find out? So being her friend who cared and I came into some money to help, I did. I sent her to one of the best rehabs in California, and she still lives there now, and she has a family and has been clean for the past two years. And she chooses not to communicate with the family. She blames them for parts of her addiction. Here are letters and pictures."

Audrey is so shocked she couldn't do anything but hugged him tightly and cry how sorry she was and that she should have let him explain instead of listening to someone like Michelle.

Audrey says, "At the movie theater, I saw a girl in the bathroom, and she said she was glad that she left you."

He says, "No, she couldn't have been talking about me. I honestly don't know who you're talking about."

Audrey confesses that she has a secret and she is sorry for not saying something sooner.

Darrelle is nervous and says, "Okay, is it bad?"

She says, "Depends on how you will take it."

He says, "Okay, honey, we can work through it. I love you, and I am all in, of course."

She pauses and says, "I hope you love me like you say because"—she pauses again—"I don't believe in abortions."

Darrelle says, "What abor—wait…are you…are you trying to tell me that I'm going to be a father?"

She says, "Yes, Darrelle."

"*Ooh, hell, yeah, yes, yes.*" He kisses her face. "I love you. How are you? Are you okay? Why have you been crying with the baby? Oh my god, I can't believe I'm about to be a father. Thank you, God. I love you, God. Did you tell your family yet? Did you tell them about the engagement?"

She says, "No."

He says, "Okay, we're going to plan a big party at our house with both of our families and announce both. How does that sound? Baby, what's wrong? Why aren't you saying anyth—"

She throws up on his shirt and says, "Sorry, honey."

"Yes, that's fine."

He takes her in the house to get cleaned up, and she gathers a few things to go and stay with him.

—⚬—

After getting in the house, Darrelle calls a doctor to stop by to check on Audrey and the baby. He is so excited. This is their first time in the situation, so he doesn't know how to help her. He has called the doctor to make sure they were okay and what can he do to help her.

They lounge on the sofa with a bucket until the doctor comes, and they discuss what sex they preferred and if they wanted to know the gender or not. They also discuss what will be the baby's name.

Audrey felt so sick but looking at Darrelle in the moment and the life and joyfulness in his face, she was content. Her life and the direction in which it is going, she can't wait to see what happens next.

Thank you Supporters

Thank you to everyone who gave my imagination a chance. I am grateful that you chose to grab my book and give it a chance. I hope that I can continue to keep you entertained with more projects of mine to come. Check me out on all my social media platforms it will be greatly appreciated.